CENTAUR

APEX

By Christine Ha

WWW.APEXEDITIONS.COM

Apex is distributed by North Star Editions:
sales@northstareditions.com | 888-417-0195

Produced for Apex by Red Line Editorial.

Photographs ©: Shutterstock Images, cover, 1, 6, 8–9, 10–11, 12, 13, 14–15, 16–17, 18–19, 22–23, 24–25, 29; L. A. Schou/Statens Museum for Kunst, 4–5; iStockphoto, 7, 20–21, 26–27

Library of Congress Control Number: 2020952924

ISBN
978-1-63738-019-2 (hardcover)
978-1-63738-055-0 (paperback)
978-1-63738-124-3 (ebook pdf)
978-1-63738-091-8 (hosted ebook)

Printed in the United States of America
Mankato, MN
082021

NOTE TO PARENTS AND EDUCATORS

Apex books are designed to build literacy skills in striving readers. Exciting, high-interest content attracts and holds readers' attention. The text is carefully leveled to allow students to achieve success quickly. Additional features, such as bolded glossary words for difficult terms, help build comprehension.

TABLE OF CONTENTS

CHAPTER 1

THE HUNT

Centaurs stand on a tall hill. Some carry giant rocks. Others have clubs made of big branches. Several boars **graze** down below.

Art and stories about centaurs often involve hunting.

The centaurs sprint down the hill.
They scream and cheer as they run.
Their hooves kick up dirt and grass.
Each step thumps like a drum.

Stories about centaurs have changed over time.

A statue in Austria shows a centaur playing a horn. Horns can be used for hunting or making music.

CHANGING STORIES

In early stories, centaurs tend to be wild. They are strong but not very smart. In later stories, centaurs are more intelligent. Many are good at **archery**.

The boars try to run. But it's too late. The centaurs catch them all.

The hunt is a success! The centaurs will eat well tonight.

In modern stories, centaurs are often skilled warriors.

Centaurs appear in many TV shows, movies, and books.

CHAPTER 2

HALF HORSE

A centaur is human from the waist up. It has the body and legs of a horse.

Centaurs have tall bodies with strong muscles.

Centaurs come from Greek **myths**. The first centaur was the son of an evil king.

In early stories, centaurs are often wild and lawless.

Greek myths link the hippocampus with Poseidon, the god of the sea.

SEA HORSE

The hippocampus is another half-horse beast. It has the upper body of a horse. Its lower half is a fish.

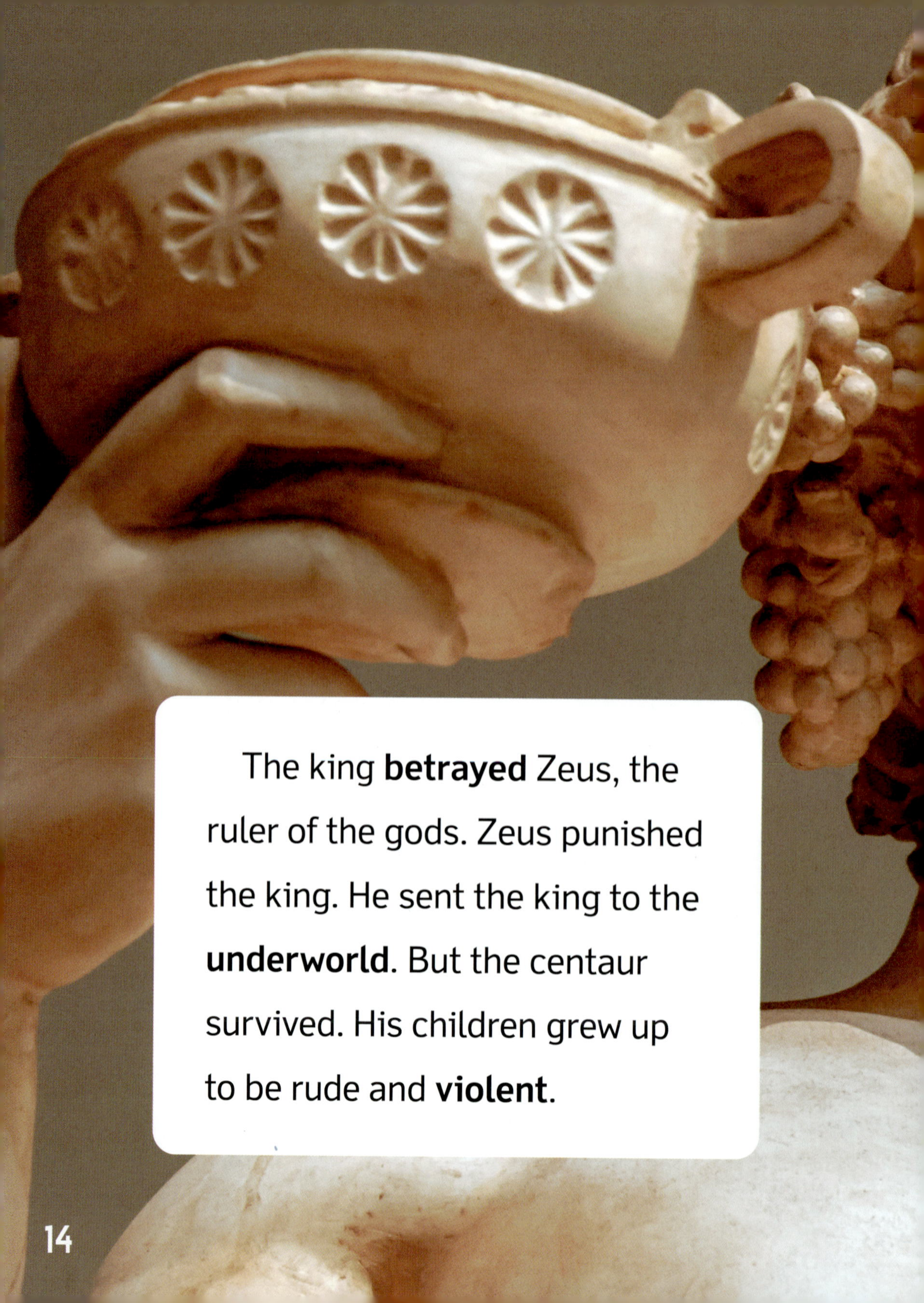

The king **betrayed** Zeus, the ruler of the gods. Zeus punished the king. He sent the king to the **underworld**. But the centaur survived. His children grew up to be rude and **violent**.

Some stories link centaurs to Dionysus, the Greek god of wine.

In Greek myths, most centaurs are male. But female centaurs appear in some art and stories.

CHAPTER 3

WILD OR WISE

According to legends, centaurs live in Thessaly. This region is in northern Greece. Centaurs **roam** its mountains, caves, and forests.

The region of Thessaly appears in several Greek myths. One is the birth of the hero Achilles.

In Greek myths, centaurs often behave badly. They start wild fights. Some even try to kidnap people.

The hero Hercules fought a wicked centaur.

One legend tells of centaurs that have horns like bulls. They live on the island of Cyprus.

The centaur Chiron taught the hero Achilles how to use a bow.

But not all centaurs are violent. Chiron is an example. He was very wise. He helped and taught many great heroes. He also had the power to heal.

STARS IN THE SKY

Centaurus is a **constellation** in the night sky. One legend says it honors Chiron. The story says the gods placed him in the stars after he died.

CHAPTER 4

TALES OF GREAT RIDERS

The people of Thessaly may have **inspired** legends of centaurs. The Thessalians raised horses.

Riding horses became an important part of life in ancient Greece and the surrounding areas.

They were skilled riders. In one sport, a man chased a bull while riding a horse. When he got close to the bull, he jumped onto its back. He grabbed its horns. Then he wrestled it to the ground.

HORSE HISTORY

The Thessalians didn't invent horseback riding. People in Central Asia had tamed horses by 3500 BCE. The Greeks started riding horses more than 1,000 years after that.

The Minoan people of Crete had a sport known as bull leaping.

People may have seen Thessalians riding. These people may not have seen horses before. They may have thought the riders were monsters.

Greek soldiers began using horses around 1500 BCE. The horses pulled chariots. Riding came later.

Greek soldiers began riding horses into battle in 900 BCE.

COMPREHENSION QUESTIONS

Write your answers on a separate piece of paper.

1. Write a paragraph explaining how legends of centaurs may have started.

2. If you made a creature that was half horse, what would the other half be? Why?

3. How was Chiron different from the other centaurs?

- **A.** He was meaner than other centaurs.
- **B.** He was bigger than other centaurs.
- **C.** He was helpful and wise.

4. How would naming a constellation after Chiron honor him?

- **A.** People would forget all about him.
- **B.** People would remember him when they studied the sky.
- **C.** The constellation would keep him from ever dying.

5. What does **sprint** mean in this book?

*The centaurs **sprint** down the hill. They scream and cheer as they run.*

A. to run quickly
B. to move slowly
C. to speak quietly

6. What does **behave** mean in this book?

*In Greek myths, centaurs often **behave** badly. They start wild fights.*

A. to not do something
B. to eat lots of food
C. to act in a certain way

Answer key on page 32.

GLOSSARY

archery
The skill of shooting arrows with a bow.

betrayed
Hurt a person or group by joining the enemy side.

chariots
Two-wheeled carts pulled by horses or other animals.

constellation
A group of stars that form a shape.

graze
To eat grass or other plants growing in a field.

inspired
Started or gave the idea for something.

myths
Well-known stories from the past that often include magic.

roam
To move throughout a large area.

underworld
The land of the dead.

violent
Likely to use physical force to hurt or attack.

TO LEARN MORE

BOOKS

Buckey, A. W. *Greek Gods, Heroes, and Mythology.* Minneapolis: Abdo Publishing, 2019.

Sautter, A. J. *Discover Gnomes, Halflings, and Other Wondrous Fantasy Beings.* Mankato, MN: Capstone Press, 2018.

Troupe, Thomas Kingsley. *Centaurs.* Minneapolis: Bellwether Media, 2021.

ONLINE RESOURCES

Visit **www.apexeditions.com** to find links and resources related to this title.

ABOUT THE AUTHOR

Christine Ha lives in Minnesota. She enjoys reading mythology and urban legends from around the world.

INDEX

Answer Key:
1. Answers will vary; **2.** Answers will vary; **3.** C; **4.** B; **5.** A; **6.** C